There are very few complete tales about the
Loch Ness Monster, but there are plenty of tales
set around Loch Ness. The story of the doors under
Urquhart Castle can be found in Constance Frederica
Gordon Cumming's In the Hebrides, 1883 and
Otta Swire's The Highlands and Their Legends, 1963.

To my brother and my cousins – Alan, Fiona, Jenny, Iain, Lorraine
– remembering all the magic, stories and games we shared at
our grandma's in Inverness — L.D.

To Hayden, Lorenza and my family. Thank you for your support,
and for filling my world with magic — N.I.

THE TREASURE OF THE LOCH NESS MONSTER

STORY BY
LARI DON

ILLUSTRATIONS BY
NATAŠA ILINČIĆ

Once upon a time, two children sat by the deep gleaming waters of Loch Ness and listened to their tummies rumble.

"I'm hungry," said Kenneth. "Are you hungry?"

Ishbel nodded. "And Granny's cupboard is empty, so we'll be hungry all winter."

Ishbel looked across the calm loch towards the ruins of Urquhart Castle. "If we found the treasure under the castle, we could buy food. Oats for porridge, wheat for bread, tatties and neeps for soup. Maybe even sugar for cakes!"

Kenneth smiled. "Don't be daft. There's no treasure under Urquhart Castle."

"Don't you remember the old story? About two doors hidden in the rock? Behind one door there's a room full of poison, behind the other there's a room full of treasure!"

"That's just a story. It's not real. It's no more real than the big green monster our great-grandpa thought he saw in the loch when he was wee."

"But some stories *are* real." Ishbel jumped up. "Unless you have a better idea for filling our porridge bowls, let's go and look for those doors."

The cousins rowed their family's old boat across the deep gleaming waters of the loch. They dragged it onto the pebbly shore under the castle ruins and stared at the blank rock.

"There are no doors," said Kenneth. "No doors, and a long row back home..."

"They're *hidden* doors." Ishbel patted the rock. "We have to search for them."

"Even if you found them, how would you choose which one to open?" asked Kenneth. "That's the point of the story, isn't it? To win the treasure, you have to risk the poison."

Ishbel ran her hands along the rock. "Our whole family is starving, so I'll take that risk."

Kenneth laughed. "That's a brave thing to say, when you haven't found any doors!"

They heard a distant splash. A wave sped across the surface of the water and sloshed against Kenneth's boots.

As the wave washed back down to the loch, the pebbles rolled away to reveal …

"A key?" Kenneth held up the brass key. "Em... Ishbel? Look what I found."

It was covered in grit, so he polished it with his sleeve.

The key glittered, and two arched doorways appeared in the rock.

"The doors are real," whispered Ishbel. "So the treasure must be real."

"And the poison," murmured Kenneth. "The poison must be real too."

"Which door will we open? Left or right?" Ishbel frowned. "We don't have a coin to toss."

"If we had a coin to toss, we wouldn't need to hunt for treasure."

Ishbel picked up a flat stone. "Light side for right, dark side for left." She threw the stone into the air and caught it. "Dark! So... left."

She took the key from Kenneth. "I'll open the door. You stay safely back."

Kenneth sighed. "No. We'll do this together."

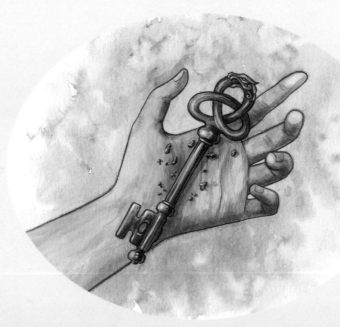

Ishbel turned the key in the lock.
They both pulled gently and the doors
creaked open.
   Through the narrow gap, they saw
a glowing yellow light.

"Gold!" gasped Ishbel.

The light thickened and swirled.

"That's not gold!" yelled Kenneth. "That's poison!"

Tendrils of sickly yellow mist oozed through the gap and wafted round Ishbel's hand.

The cousins crashed their shoulders against the doors, slamming them shut. The mist vanished.

Ishbel locked the doors. "My fingers are itchy." She wiped them on her skirt. "But now we've found the poison, we know where to find the treasure."

Ishbel turned the key in the other lock. They both
pulled cautiously and the doors creaked open.

There was no yellow light, just a puff of dust.

They hauled the doors wide open. The stone chamber
was filled with ancient armour, broken battleaxes,
torn tapestries and …

"Gold!" shouted Ishbel, as they rushed forward.

"Golden eggs!" Kenneth lifted one. "They're very heavy."

"We can buy lots of food with these!" Ishbel grinned.

"Granny's cupboard will be full, and we'll never be hungry again!"

They carried the eggs, one by one, to the boat.

As Kenneth collected the last egg, he noticed a gold coin below a beautiful tapestry. He picked it up and put it in his pocket.

Ishbel blew on her fingers, which had started to throb.

As Kenneth placed the egg in the boat, Ishbel turned the key in the lock.

And the doors faded away.

Ishbel and Kenneth rowed
across the calm water.
When they reached
the middle of the deep
gleaming loch, Ishbel said,
"My skin is burning."

She stopped rowing and dangled
her hand over the side of the boat,
to cool her fingers.

Beneath her, she glimpsed a
vast curved shape.

She saw the surface of the
loch tremble.

She felt the boat rock.

A huge green head shot up from the
depths of Loch Ness and crashed into
the bottom of the boat.
The wooden boat flew into the air.
It splintered and split and broke apart.

Kenneth, Ishbel, the golden
eggs and the brass key tumbled
into Loch Ness. They sank into
the deep cold water.

Down below, the cousins saw the long
green beast who had attacked their boat.

She was curving and coiling through the water, gathering the bright eggs in a loop of her tail and rolling them onto a ledge. Ishbel and Kenneth kicked upwards to the surface.

"Did you see the monster?" spluttered Kenneth. "Did you see her saving the eggs?"

Ishbel coughed. "Maybe that's why she broke our boat, to get her eggs back?"

Kenneth looked across the wide loch. "We're a long way from home." He looked over his wet shoulder. "And a long way from the castle. I don't think I can swim that far."

"Neither can I," said Ishbel. "And that great big monster is probably still under us right now…"

Ishbel and Kenneth started to wave wildly at the shore shouting: "Help! Please! Help!"

Suddenly Kenneth and Ishbel felt something solid rise up under them.

The huge green beast was lifting them out of the cold water.

They shivered and clutched each other.

Then the great green creature began to swim across the loch, and Ishbel whispered, "I think … she's taking us … home!"

So the cousins sat still and calm, perched high on the curved back of the beast, as she carried them across Loch Ness.

When the huge green beast reached the shore, Kenneth and Ishbel slid off her back. As she turned and swam away, three elegant curves rose up then dived down.

Ishbel rubbed her hand. The cold water had eased the pain, but there were still yellow marks under her skin. She wondered if they would ever fade.

"The magical stories are true!" said Kenneth. "Let's tell everyone that we found Urquhart Castle's treasure and Great-Grandpa's monster!"

"No one would believe us. The doors and key have disappeared, and that beautiful beast can hide deep in the loch." Ishbel sighed. "She rescued her eggs and she rescued us. But we lost the treasure."

"Not *all* the treasure…" Kenneth pulled the gold coin from his pocket.

Ishbel gasped. "Our own small treasure! Enough to buy food for the winter, and maybe even a couple of cakes!"

As the cousins ran home, a long green tail waved,
then vanished…

…into the deep gleaming waters of Loch Ness.